KU-180-691

WITHDRAWN

A000 000 002 5791
ABERDEEN LIBRARIES

"When I was a pirate I could run 100 metres quicker than you can say doubloon," says Gran, "especially with a policeman after me."

So Gran's invited her old shipmates Flint-Hearted Jack, Fingers O'Malley and Cut-throat Malone to help her train for the Olympics.

I heard her shout "Avast there me hearties" when they were running round the garden baton-passing this afternoon but **someone** kept dropping it.

Gran's very loyal so she won't say **who**, but I notice she's been calling the bosun **Butterfingers** O'Malley.

She's knitted special striped costumes for the synchronised swimming, and she and her pet crocodile have already made quite a splash at the pool.

Mind you, when she saw the headline *Man-eater Terrifies Toddlers* in the paper Gran was **furious.**

"My pet crocodile is good with children, and has never eaten anyone who didn't deserve it," said Gran.

I think her jumping looks
very promising.

She's been using the clothes prop to pole-vault over the washing line . . .

. . . and land in the compost heap.

"It's one small step for a Gran," she said dusting off the cabbage leaves, "one giant leap for Grankind."

Of course pole-vaulting isn't for everyone, but Gran says if you don't mind feeling dizzy and showing your knickers it's a sport more Grans should think about.

Grandpa banned bowling after one of Gran's cannon balls blew up his greenhouse.

With him in it.

BOOM
BANG

"Lot of fuss about nothing," Gran grumbled after she'd rescued him. "The day I can't haul an old man out of an apple tree is the day I hang up my flintlock."

But even Grandpa admits she is **brilliant** at showjumping – although it is the first time he's seen it done on a crocodile.

There's no doubt Gran's a crack shot with her blunderbuss.

"Show me a varmint at 50 paces, and I'll show you a man with a hole through his hat," laughed Gran after she'd fired at Grandpa's scarecrow.

She's **really** good at fencing too.

Grandpa challenged her to a duel with a cucumber...

and Gran sliced it into
sandwiches with her cutlass.

And she's claiming the world record for the fastest Gran over 800 metres –

although Grandpa still says it
doesn't count if you have been
fired out of a cannon.

I'd love to see Gran standing under a Jolly Roger listening to a sea shanty when she gets a gold medal.

But Gran says the most important thing isn't winning, it's taking part and having fun.

So just in case Grandpa is going to make her a special medal from all of us – for being the world's Champion Gran.

3
1
2
5
6

For my crew: Patrick & Jimmy, Barnaby & Julia, Toby & Jo, Jez & Becca, Eleanor & Alice.

The first book of Pirate Gran was developed from the winning entry to the BBC London / RaW 60-second story-writing competition. RaW is the BBC's biggest ever campaign to help adults across the UK to build their confidence in reading and writing, by telling stories to their children.

All rights reserved.

No part of this publication may be produced, stored or introduced into a retrieval system, or transmitted, in any form, or by any means (electronic, mechanical, photocopying, recording or otherwise) without the prior written permission of the publisher. Any person who does any unauthorised act in relation to this publication may be liable to criminal prosecution and civil claims for damages.

A CIP catalogue record for this book is available from The British Library.

First published in the UK in 2010 by the National Maritime Museum, Greenwich, London SE10 9NF

www.nmm.ac.uk/publishing

Text © 2010 Geraldine Durrant and illlustrations © 2010 Rose Forshall

Design Kayt Manson and project management Sara Ayad

Hardback 978-1-906367-47-3

Paperback 978-1-906367-48-0

Printed in China